Jonathan the pony had a **very** special talent.

With one wave of his wand,
he could make **anything** disappear.

Watch this . . .

See!
The frog! It's gone!

But don't worry.
Because whenever Jonathan
waved his wand again . . .

3... 2... 1...

. . . everything came back.

BOOOMF!

(Phew.)

Everything always came back,
because Jonathan was a
brilliant magician.

So when Jonathan the Magic Pony
made Sarah's bear disappear –

BOOMF!

It came straight back.
Except . . .

"That's not my bear," said Sarah.
"My bear is red. This bear is blue."

"Oh," said Jonathan.

"Well, not to worry. These things happen sometimes."

He raised his wand high in the air,
and . . .

BOOOMF!

"That's not my bear either," said Sarah.
"That's a duck."

"I know it's a duck!" said Jonathan. "It's part of the trick!

And now for your bear –

3... 2... 1..."

BOOMF!

"No," said Sarah.
"That's a shark. Are you *sure* you're a magician?"

"Oh yes, definitely a magician," said Jonathan quickly.
"What a show this is! Now here's your bear!

3... 2... 1..."

BOOMF!

"No,
that's a moth."

BOOMF!

"No, that's a sloth."

BOOMF!

"That's a lamb!"

BOOMF!

"That's a clam!"

BOOMF!

"That's a **calf**!"

BOOOMF!

"That's a **giraffe**!"

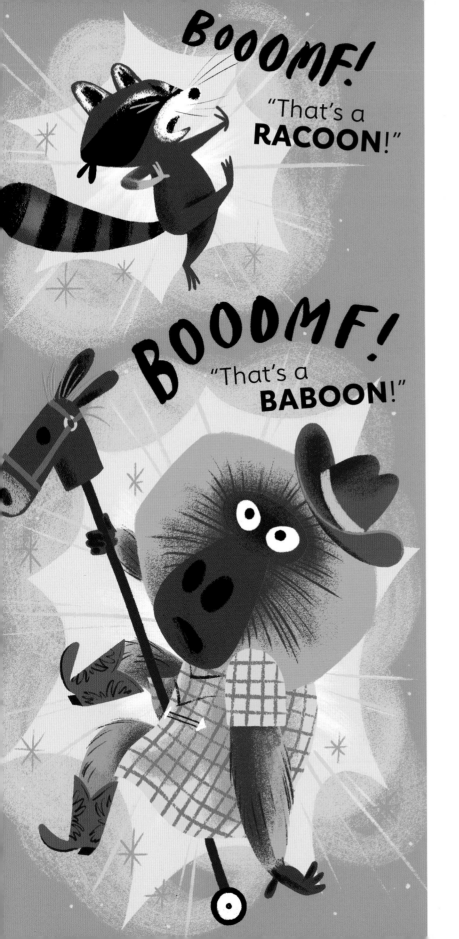

BOOOMF!

"That's a **RACOON!**"

BOOOMF!

"That's a **BABOON!**"

"And **THAT's** a wooden spoon!"

PAFF!

It was the last straw.

I WANT

MY BEAR!

shouted Sarah.

Jonathan closed his eyes and took a deep breath.
It was a very important moment.

No.
It was a chimpanzee.
Covered in fleas.

"You are **not**
a good magician!"
cried Sarah.

Just then, a flea jumped on to Jonathan's nose.

"Get off!" he shouted.
"It tickles!"

Jonathan started to sneeze –

ah... ah... AH...

BOOOOOOOMF!

Whoops.

Jonathan's sneeze had made everything disappear.
Even Jonathan.

But not Sarah.
　　The wand was still there too.

Sarah looked at it.
What should she do?

It worked!

"You found my bear!"
said Sarah.

"No, YOU found your bear," said Jonathan.

Sarah laughed.
"Turns out *I'm* the magician!" she said.

"Oh, fine," said Jonathan.
"Magic is rubbish. And anyway . . ."

"I want to be a **SUPERHERO!**"